This book belongs to:

JORDON XU

Digital art by Callaway Animation Studios under the direction of David Kirk
in collaboration with Nelvana Limited.

This book is based on the TV episode "I'll Fly Away," written by Nadine Van Der Velde,
from the animated TV series *Miss Spider's Sunny Patch Friends* on Nick Jr.,
a Nelvana Limited/Absolute Pictures Limited co-production in association
with Callaway Arts & Entertainment, based on the Miss Spider books by David Kirk.

Nicholas Callaway, President and Publisher
Cathy Ferrara, Managing Editor and Production Director
Antoinette White, Senior Editor • Toshiya Masuda, Art Director
George Gould, Director of Digital Services • Joya Rajadhyaksha, Associate Editor
Doug Vitarelli, Director of Animation • Raphael Shea, Art Assistant • Cara Paul, Digital Artist
Amy Cloud, Assistant Editor • Krupa Jhaveri, Design Assistant • Alex Ballas, Design Assistant
Keith McMenamy, Digital Artist • Masako Ebata, Designer

Special thanks to the Nelvana staff, including Doug Murphy, Scott Dyer, Tracy Ewing, Pam Lehn,
Tonya Lindo, Mark Picard, Susie Grondin, Luis Lopez, Eric Pentz, and Georgina Robinson.

Library of Congress Cataloging-in-Publication Data available upon request.

Distributed in the United States by Penguin Young Readers Group.

Callaway Arts & Entertainment, its Callaway logotype,
and Callaway & Kirk Company LLC are trademarks.

ISBN 978-0-448-45007-0

Visit Callaway Arts & Entertainment at www.callaway.com.

10 9 8 7 6 5 4 3 2 1 08 09 10

Printed in China

I'll Fly Away

David Kirk

CALLAWAY

NEW YORK

2008

Everybuggy in Sunny Patch was so excited. The Flying Aces were in town! Dragon couldn't wait to see Rocky and Roxie, the leaders of the troop.

High in the sky, the Aces
flew forwards and backwards.
They did figure eights and
loop-de-loops.

"Buggin'!" gasped Dragon.
"I wish *I* could do that!"

Rocky landed on a nearby tree stump.

"Howdy kids! Who wants to get a taste of the sky?"

All the little bugs raised their arms. The Aces invited Bounce to come for a ride.

"Be careful with Bounce!" Dragon exclaimed. "We've been through everything together. We're best bug buddies for life!"

"You should join our school," Rocky said. "With a little practice, you could be a Flying Ace in no time!"

"Really? *Me*?" cried Dragon.

That night Dragon told his mom he wanted to join the Flying Aces.

"I don't think so, Dragon," said Miss Spider. "You're a part of our family now. You can fly away some other day."

Dragon sighed and slumped off to bed.

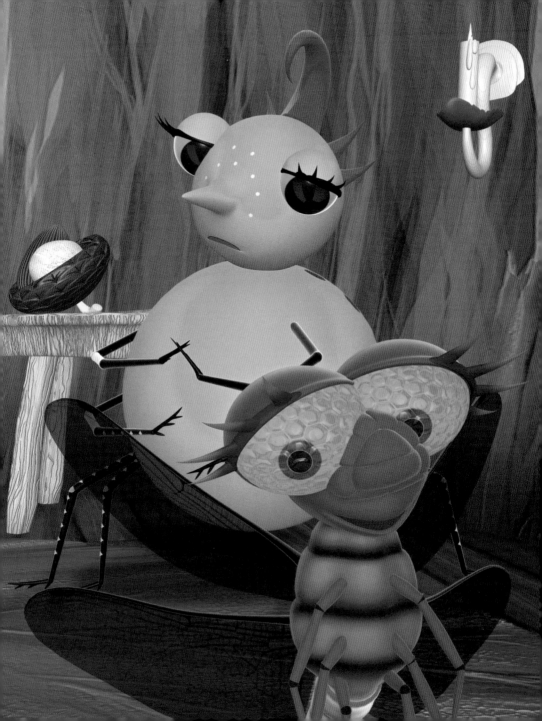

Dragon couldn't sleep.

"Are you leaving us?" asked a tearful Bounce. "I thought we were best bug buddies for life."

"We are," said Dragon, "but I'm a dragonfly. I should be with other dragonflies!"

The next day, Miss Spider and Holley discussed what Dragon had said.

"Maybe he's right," sighed Miss Spider. "Maybe he does belong with other dragonflies."

Though they didn't want to let Dragon go, they decided to let him follow his dreams.

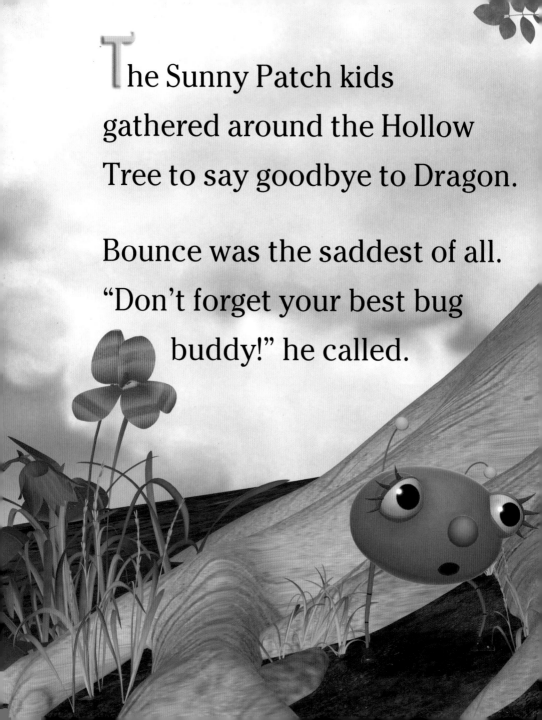

The Sunny Patch kids gathered around the Hollow Tree to say goodbye to Dragon.

Bounce was the saddest of all. "Don't forget your best bug buddy!" he called.

Miss Spider and Holley
gave Dragon a final squeeze.
"We love you, Dragon,"
they said.

Dragon squeezed them
back. "I love you too," he
said. Then, looking at the
clouds, he took off to meet
Rocky and Roxie.

Dragon practiced his moves with the Aces. He learned to fly in formation, to make beautiful figure eights, and a perfect loop-de-loop. But he didn't feel happy. He couldn't stop thinking about his family.

At the Dribbly Dell, Squirt, Shimmer, and Bounce were trying to start a soccerberry game. But without their star player Dragon, it wasn't much fun.

Suddenly, they heard the sound of wings.

"Dragon's back!" yelled Bounce.

"But Dragon," began Holley, "you wanted to be with other dragonflies!"

"I thought I did," replied Dragon. "They may be dragonflies, but you're my family."

Everyone cheered.
The happy family
was together again.